THE KING AND I

ADAPTED BY BONNIE BADER
FROM THE ANIMATED MOTION PICTURE ADAPTED FROM THE MUSICAL
BY RICHARD RODGERS AND OSCAR HAMMERSTEIN II.

Scholastic Inc.
New York Toronto London Auckland Sydney Mexico City New Delhi Hong Kong

No part of this publication may be reproduced in whole or in part, or stored in a retrieval system, or transmitted in any form or by any means, electronic, mechanical, photocopying, recording, or otherwise, without written permission of the publisher. For information regarding permission, write to Scholastic Inc., Attention: Permissions Department, 555 Broadway, New York, NY 10012.

For all lyrics from Rodgers and Hammerstein's THE KING AND I contained herein:
Copyright © 1951 by Richard Rodgers and Oscar Hammerstein II. Copyright Renewed. WILLIAMSON MUSIC owner of publication and allied rights throughout the world. International Copyright Secured. All Rights Reserved, Printed by Permission.

The King & I is a trademark used under license from the Rodgers and Hammerstein organization on behalf of the Rodgers family partnership and the estate of Oscar Hammerstein II.

ISBN 0-590-68066-8

© 1999 by Morgan Creek Productions, Inc.
All rights reserved. Published by Scholastic Inc.
SCHOLASTIC and associated logos are trademarks and/or registered trademarks of Scholastic Inc.

12 11 10 9 8 7 6 5 4 3 2   9/9 0 1 2 3 4/0

Designed by Madalina Stefan

Printed in the U.S.A.
First Scholastic printing, March 1999

THE ARRIVAL

Twelve-year-old Louis Leonowens was sailing on a ship in the gulf of Siam along with his mother, Anna. Anna was going to be the schoolteacher for the royal children of Siam.

Louis looked out to sea. The waves were breaking high and hard, and the sky was darkening. He clutched a railing with one hand, desperately trying to keep his balance on the rocking ship. In his other hand he held out a biscuit. "Moonshee, please come back," Louis cried to a monkey that was clinging to the bowsprit at the front of the boat.

Overhead, a storm brewed ominously; the sun was covered by a swirling mist. Louis's eyes widened, but he swallowed hard and quickly tied a rope around his waist. He had to reach Moonshee before he fell overboard!

The ship tossed wildly. Suddenly, a big wave swept them both away!

Meanwhile, Louis's mother, Anna, was in her cabin when she saw something sweeping by her porthole.

"Louis?!" Anna cried, rushing up to the deck.

As soon as she reached the deck, Louis had pulled himself back on board.

"Moonshee was frightened," Louis tried to explain to his mother.

Suddenly, the wild wind lashed at Anna's umbrella, turning it inside out. The boat tilted violently, and Moonshee started to slide overboard again. Louis lunged and scooped up the little monkey.

"Louis! Watch out!" Anna cried, desperately trying to save her son. Somehow she managed to catch him and bring him in. "I was so afraid," she whispered.

4

Inside his chamber in Bangkok, Siam, the King's prime minister, the evil Kralahome, watched Anna and Louis in his magical gong.

The Kralahome was a magician and he could create illusions to scare people. This time he was planning to scare Anna. "I'll have her shivering in her shoes!" the Kralahome told his assistant, Master Little.

The Kralahome was scheming behind the King's back. His plan was to scare Anna into believing that the King was evil and should be deposed. And the Kralahome had just the person in mind to take the King's place — himself!

The Kralahome commanded Master Little to strike the gong. In the gong's image, the clouds around the ship seethed and boiled.

5

A mass of storm clouds swirled over the ship. But the Kralahome had turned the clouds into a horrifying sea serpent. It roared thunderously, shooting tendrils of smoke from its mouth that whipped around Anna's and Louis's legs.

"Mother, does anything ever frighten you?" Louis asked, nervously eyeing the serpent.

"Sometimes," Anna confessed.

"What do you do?" Louis wanted to know.

"I whistle." Anna stood up straight, pursed her lips, and began to whistle. Then she began to sing:

Whenever I feel afraid
I hold my head erect
And whistle a happy tune,
So no one will suspect
          I'm afraid.

Louis began to whistle, too, and their fears soon disappeared.

FIRST ENCOUNTER

Finally, Anna and Louis arrived in Bangkok. The Kralahome met them at the ship, and escorted them to the royal palace, where they were to meet the King.

The towering gold doors of the royal palace, flanked by two massive marble elephants, swung open. The Kralahome led Anna and Louis across a beautiful courtyard and down a long hallway toward the throne room.

Once they reached the throne room, Anna and Louis peered inside. There sat the King upon his throne. He stroked his black panther, Rama, sitting regally beside him. Behind the throne was an array of presents that had been given to the King — rugs, vases, painted scrolls, and a clock.

7

Anna and Louis watched as a Burmese nobleman, wearing an elaborate turban decorated with jeweled fruit, approached the throne. He pulled a young girl alongside him.

"Burma sends a gift to the King of Siam," the Kralahome explained to Anna and Louis.

"Gift?" Anna asked, confused.

"Sometimes rugs. Once, a cuckoo clock. This time, *her*," the Kralahome said.

"That *girl*?" Anna said, outraged. "She's a person, not a rug!"

"Tell the King what useful thing you can do," the Burmese nobleman commanded the girl.

"I can read, Your Majesty," Tuptim answered.

"In Siam books are forbidden to servants!" the King roared.

Anna could not believe her ears. Being forbidden to read?!

Tuptim's lips began to tremble, but she held her head proudly.

"Infinite pardons, Your Majesty," the emissary said. "She can arrange flowers."

Suddenly, Moonshee leaped onto the nobleman's head. He thought the fruit on his turban was real, but it was really made of precious stones. Moonshee ran away with a handful of jewels. Palace guards sprang forward, wielding swords, trying to capture Moonshee.

Louis chased after Moonshee, desperately trying to save him. He clamped his foot down, snagging the monkey's leash. But when he looked up, he came face-to-face with a sword-wielding guard!

Anna raced to protect Louis.

"Who? Who? Who?" the King cried out, clapping his hands.

"Your Majesty, he meant no harm. . . ." Anna began.

The King cut her off with a wave of his hand, and stepped down from his throne. "Never hide behind a woman's skirt," the King told Louis. "It is not very brave. Also, impossible to know when she will sit down."

Then the King pointed to Anna.

"I am Anna Leonowens, Your Majesty, the schoolteacher you sent for," Anna began.

"Yes, yes. You are part of my plan, bringing what is good in Western culture to Siam. Come!"

And with that, he grabbed Anna's arm and pulled her away.

The King took Anna to his science lab and proudly gave her a tour. He showed her his printing press, a collection of fireworks, and a model balloon.

But Anna had a question for the King. She had been promised her own home outside the palace. So far, no mention had been made of that. She asked the King again.

The King did not answer her. Instead, he shouted out a command: "Have the children prepare for the presentation."

Anna was furious. "I want my house! The house I was promised, Your Majesty."

Finally, the King answered. "You teach in the palace, you shall live in the palace!" And with that, His Royal Highness stormed out.

THE PRINCE AND THE SERVANT GIRL

Out in the palace garden, Tuptim stared into a pond. A teardrop fell on her reflection.

All of a sudden, something nuzzled her hair. Startled, she turned around and saw a small elephant with a broken tusk.

"Some hunter, I bet, did this to you," Tuptim said to the elephant with a smile. "How about I call you Tusker?" She picked a banana from a tree and gave it to the elephant, tossing away the peel.

Just then, Tuptim heard a shout. She peered through the bushes and saw two kick boxers practicing. She watched the two young men for a while. Then, one of them slipped and fell on the banana peel!

"Are you hurt?" Tuptim asked, going over to the fallen man. Her heart skipped a beat when she saw him.

"Just my pride," the young man answered sheepishly. "Who are you?" He suddenly had to know who this beautiful young woman was.

"A mere 'object' given to the King," Tuptim answered, hanging her head. "Are you a soldier?" she wondered.

"I-I-I serve the King," the young man stammered.

"That makes two of us," Tuptim told the young man. "Two servants."

Tuptim and the young man stared at each other. They had fallen in love at first sight!

Inside the palace, Anna walked into her apartment to find the ladies of the court unpacking her clothing. But Anna told them she was not staying.

The women were curious about Anna. Some of them came over to her and peered under her hoopskirt.

"They wonder why you wear tent, Mrs. Anna," Lady Thiang explained. "They think you're shaped like that."

Anna laughed and lifted her dress. "Look, two legs."

Another woman took a small, framed photo from Anna's suitcase. She wanted to know if the man in the picture was Anna's husband. Anna smiled and took back the photo. She wandered over to the window and saw Tuptim and the young man in the garden. She realized instantly the two had fallen for each other.

"Servant girl and Crown Prince is forbidden," Lady Thiang, who had followed Anna to the window, said. "Against tradition!"

But Anna secretly hoped that the Prince and Tuptim would be strong enough to follow their dreams.

THE MARCH OF THE SIAMESE CHILDREN

Inside the throne room, everyone gathered for the presentation.
"The children come for presentment," the King told Anna.
"Your Majesty . . ." Anna began, "I'm not staying. . . ."
"Silence!" the King cried out.
Anna had no choice but to stand and watch the presentation. One by one, the children entered. Princess Kannika, Princess Naomi, Prince Ratsami, Princess Manya, identical twins Prince Thoni and Prince Moni, and six-year-old Princess Ying, the youngest of the royal children. Then Crown Prince

Chululongkorn came in. Anna recognized him as the kick boxer in the garden. The children bowed before the King, crossed over to Anna, and touched her hands to their foreheads as a sign of respect.

Finally, the procession ended and all the children were kneeling. Anna looked at all their faces and sighed.

"Our schoolteacher has changed her mind," the King announced. "Will live in palace."

"For the time being, Your Majesty," Anna replied.

It was nighttime. Inside the royal elephant stables, the Kralahome commanded Master Little to take a letter. He was not happy that Anna had chosen to stay, so he decided to write a letter to the British diplomat — a letter filled with lies. The Kralahome hoped that once the diplomat read the letter, he'd come to Siam and release the King from power.

"To Sir Edward Ramsay, British envoy," the Kralahome dictated. "Your schoolteacher is in grave danger," he began. He continued on about the "evil" King.

When he was finished with the letter, he looked up at one of the elephants inside the stable and snarled, "When I start an ivory trade, you'll be the first! Your tusks will fetch a fine price."

"I thought the King won't allow the ivory trade...." Master Little began. "*Got it*, O Corporate One," he said, finally understanding.

The letter soon reached Sir Edward, who was alarmed that Anna was in danger. He decided to head straight for Siam to dethrone the barbaric King! Which was *exactly* what the Kralahome wanted!

18

GETTING TO KNOW YOU

The next day, Anna went to the palace schoolroom. All the royal children were sitting on the floor, except Prince Chululongkorn, the Crown Prince, who sat at a jeweled desk.

Anna showed the children a world map. The Crown Prince could not believe how small Siam was, especially since he thought the royal Siamese palace was the center of the whole universe!

"I suppose we all think our home is the most important place, whether we live in a palace or not," Anna said.

Then Anna discovered that the children had never even been outside the palace walls! There was so much for her to teach these children — and learn about them, too.

Anna decided to show them how other people lived, and led them to the palace gate, but the children were afraid to go outside!

Louis went through the gates first, and all the children followed.
As they walked, Anna began to sing:

Getting to know you,
Getting to know all about you,
Getting to like you,
Getting to hope you like me.
Getting to know you—
Putting it my way, but nicely,
You are precisely
my cup of tea!

Anna led the children past market stalls and temples. They watched silk
being spun and dyed. Then she led them past rice paddies where water buffalo
were plowing. The children were having a wonderful time, making new friends
everywhere they went.

Meanwhile, the Kralahome, who had seen Anna take the children outside of the palace walls, reported back to the King. He knew the King would be furious, and he was right!

When Anna and the children returned to the palace, the King was waiting for them. "You have been outside the palace?!" the King accused her.

"I thought it important they learn how people live outside the palace," Anna replied.

His Royal Highness turned to Princess Kannika and said, "Tell me something you learn?"

Princess Kannika was afraid, but she answered. "There are nice little houses outside the palace, Father."

The King thought he knew what Anna was doing. She was not going to let him forget his promise of an apartment. But Anna really just wanted to show the children life outside the palace walls. Still, His Majesty insisted that Anna stay *inside* the palace. He told her that she was his servant.

Anna was outraged. She decided to take Louis and leave Siam for good!

Still angry at Anna, the King paced back and forth in the throne room while Prince Chululongkorn tried to question him.

"Father, you seem so angry with changes; how can we be modern if you keep to old ways?" the Crown Prince asked. Deliberately, he threw in, "For example, if you were a modern scientific king, would you still choose a wife for your son?"

"Of course!" the King snapped. "How can a boy be wise enough to select a good wife?"

"It's possible," Prince Chululongkorn said.

The ruler looked at his son and saw the confusion in his eyes. He rubbed the pendant that hung around his neck, then lifted it off and slipped it over the Prince's bowed head.

The Prince could not believe that his father had given him the royal pendant. But after all, Prince Chululongkorn would be King one day.

DANGEROUS DREAMS

Later that afternoon, Louis and the Crown Prince were kick boxing in the palace garden. By luck, Louis landed a jab on the Prince's nose!

As the Prince was washing the wound, Tuptim and Tusker came up to him. "You're hurt," Tuptim said, reaching up to touch the Prince's face. Then suddenly, she gasped at the sight of the royal pendant hanging around his neck. "You're the Crown Prince?" Tuptim asked, falling to her knees.

The Prince told Tuptim that he had been afraid to reveal the truth to her. Tuptim tried to run away, but the Prince wouldn't let her. Then he sang:

I have dreamed that your arms are lovely,
I have dreamed what a joy you'll be.
I have dreamed every word you'll whisper
When you're close,
Close to me.

As a gesture of true love, the Prince put his royal pendant around Tuptim's neck. He promised to tell his father about them.

23

While Tuptim and Prince Chululongkorn were in the garden, Master Little had been hiding in the bushes, spying on them. He could not wait to tell the Kralahome what he had seen!

But Tusker had been there, too. He chased Master Little, jabbing him with his one sharp tusk. Master Little had to climb up a mango tree to safety. Tusker planned to wait at the bottom of the tree until Master Little decided to come down. It was going to be a long night!

BEST FOOT FORWARD

Anna was finishing her packing when Prince Chululongkorn came to her door. "Mrs. Anna, I am worried," the Prince began. He told Anna he had heard that letters were sent to the British saying that his father was a barbarian.

A barbarian? Anna knew that was ridiculous. She wanted to help the King — but couldn't.

"I cannot give advice without having been asked," Anna explained to the Prince.

The Prince gave Anna a pleading look, but he knew his father was a proud man and would not ask for help. Disappointed, he bowed and left her room.

But after the Prince left, Anna changed her mind. She would go speak with the King, after all.

25

Anna went to see the King in the throne room. Upon seeing her, His Royal Highness thought she had come to apologize. But Anna was determined to speak to the King about the news the Prince had brought her.

"Your Majesty," Anna began carefully, "has there been any...news... recently?"

"News?" the King said, understanding now why Anna had come. "Yes, there is news. They call me a barbarian!"

"But it's a lie!" Anna said. "What have you decided to do about it?"

"You guess what I will do. Guess!"

What Anna privately guessed was that the King was seeking her advice. She decided to give it. "I believe you'll invite the British to the palace. To show the truth by putting your best foot forward."

The King knew a good idea when he heard it. He told Anna that that was *exactly* what he had planned to do. He would entertain the British with a banquet!

26

All this time, the Kralahome had been listening in on the King and Anna. He wasn't happy with what he had heard. He went to find his sidekick.

But the Kralahome did not know that Master Little was still stuck up in the mango tree. Master Little looked down at the bottom of the tree. It seemed as if the elephant had finally left. He decided to make his getaway, when suddenly mangos came flying at him! Moonshee and Tusker pelted him with fruit all the way back to the palace.

"Where have you been?" the Kralahome demanded of Master Little when he finally arrived in his chamber.

But the roly-poly assistant was too out of breath to speak. Instead, he tried to pantomime what he had seen. He acted out that he had seen the Prince give the royal pendant to the servant girl.

"Good!" the Kralahome said, excited. "A perfect dish for the banquet. The British watching our King's every move and—*surprise!*—a servant girl has the royal pendant! What else can His Majesty do but *sentence her to a barbaric death*!"

27

Anna and the King worked very hard to prepare for the banquet. Anna picked roses to help remind their British guests of home, gave the seamstresses instructions on how to make hoopskirts for the ladies of the palace, and gave the cooks recipes for English cooking — without white-hot Siamese pepper sauce!

The King practiced eating with a fork, readied his scientific hot air balloon for a demonstration, and prepared a fireworks display.

At last, everything was ready.

Sir Edward, the British envoy, arrived. Anna and the King ushered him inside the banquet hall.

THE KRALAHOME'S REVENGE

The Kralahome sat uncomfortably at the table. He knew he had to make his move soon. When the conversation turned to elephants, the Kralahome mentioned the sacred white elephant. He said that its value is symbolized in a pendant that is worn by the King.

The King motioned to his son. "Future King. Show!"

The Prince looked trapped. He did not know what to say.

The Kralahome did. He signaled to the guards. A struggling Tuptim was brought in.

The King saw the pendant around Tuptim's neck and was furious. "Dishonor!" he yelled, ripping the pendant from Tuptim's neck. "Have her whipped, till death!"

Anna and Sir Edward were appalled. But the Kralahome was pleased. His plan to make the King look barbaric was working!

The King raised his whip, but then looked at Anna. She stood horrified at his side, and the King changed his mind. "Send her back to Burma!"

"No!" the Prince shouted. "She'll be killed!" The Prince kick boxed the nearest guard, grabbed Tuptim's hand, and fled.

All at once, Louis scooped up Moonshee and ran off after his friends.

THE CHASE

"Louis!" Anna called after her son. Then she turned to the King and shouted, "See what you've done!"

"Bring them back," the King, upset and angry, ordered the Kralahome.

The Kralahome bowed. He went off to find Master Little. "Make *sure* there's an accident this time. And bring back their bodies," the Kralahome commanded his pudgy servant.

And with that, Master Little and the guards were off in hot pursuit of Prince Chululongkorn, Tuptim, Louis, and Moonshee.

"Everything is working out perfectly, for me," the Kralahome said to himself with a grin.

The Prince, Tuptim, Louis, and Moonshee ran over the rooftops. Finally, they could run no more. They had come to the palace wall. There was a huge drop. Should they turn back? No. It was too late. The palace guards were running toward them. They were trapped!

Just then, Louis lost his balance. Prince Chululongkorn tried to grab him, but he slipped. And Tuptim, trying to save the Prince, tumbled after them over the wall.

Miraculously, none of them got hurt. Instead of crashing, they were lifted into the air by elephant trunks. Tusker and his father, the King's royal white elephant, had caught them. The four runaways fled from the palace on the elephants' backs. They rode straight into the jungle.

31

Inside his chamber, the Kralahome watched the runaways through his magic gong. He picked up the mallet and struck the gong, creating the illusion of a gigantic, scary spiderweb. The Prince, Tuptim, Louis, and Moonshee were blocked!

They turned their elephants around and fled in the opposite direction. As soon as they were gone, the "spiderweb" shrank back to its normal size.

They continued through the jungle. But suddenly, they came face-to-face with Master Little and the guards.

"Reverse!" Louis shouted. "Where's reverse?"

The runaways tried another path, only to be confronted by roaring, snarling tigers. They quickly turned in another direction. Then the tigers changed back into what they once were — little jungle mice. Just like the spiderweb, the tigers had been another of the Kralahome's tricks!

Inside the Temple of the Jade Buddha, the King was praying for guidance. "What shall I do?" the King asked with a sigh. "I cannot apologize. A king? Grovel?"

Then, an idea began to dawn upon him. "If I find the children, this will show Mrs. Anna I am sorry." The King began to come up with a plan!

34

Inside Anna's chambers, Sir Edward paced angrily by the window.

"When I make my report, the entire fleet will be dispatched," Sir Edward said. "That'll be *that* for this King of Siam!"

"Edward, please." Anna tried to reason with him. She knew the King wasn't really barbaric.

Suddenly, the King appeared at Anna's window! And he was flying in his hot air balloon. The King was going to try to rescue the children!

Finally, the Prince, Tuptim, Louis, and Moonshee came to a rickety, two-rope suspension bridge.

The Prince was the first one to try to make it across the bridge. Then Tusker. Then Tuptim. But when Louis and Moonshee went to cross, the planks of wood on the bridge began to disappear — the Kralahome had struck again!

The Prince and Tuptim tried to help, but they all fell into the raging rapids below.

Tuptim spotted a raft large enough to hold all of them. But as soon as they jumped on, the raft melted away. The Kralahome wasn't done yet!

The group quickly swam toward one of the riverbanks that was lined with logs. Only they weren't logs at all — they turned into crocodiles before their eyes!

Quickly, Louis, Moonshee, the Prince, and Tuptim swam away from the crocodiles. On the riverbank they saw a very old temple — the Ancient Place of Elephants. Everywhere they looked, they saw statues of elephants.

"What is this place?" Louis asked, his eyes open wide in amazement.

The Kralahome was about to play another trick. And without warning, the elephants sprang to life, swinging and smashing out with their trunks.

"Ah-h-h-h!" the Prince, Tuptim, Moonshee, and Louis screamed together. Before they could do anything, they were swept down the throat of a huge elephant. It felt as if they were on a wild-water roller coaster!

37

Master Little and the guards were following close behind the runaways. Suddenly, Master Little was swept into the elephant's throat, too.

But just then, Louis and the Prince were shot *out* of the elephant's mouth.

"You're safe!" Louis cried to the Prince.

But Master Little was right there with them. "Wrong!" he said, pointing a spear at them.

Louis took one look at the weapon and began to whistle.

"It's not time to whistle," the Prince told him. But Louis just continued.

"You'd better be afraid, and say good-bye, O Juvenile One," Master Little chuckled.

But just then, a giant blast of water knocked down Master Little! It was Tusker and his father the white elephant, to the rescue again, blasting water from their trunks!

Tuptim came shooting out of the elephant's mouth, into the raging river.
"Get her!" the Prince cried.

The Prince, Louis, and Moonshee raced off on the elephants' backs, along the riverbank.

Desperately, they tried to reach Tuptim. They came to a giant cliff where the river plunged into a hole at the bottom. If Tuptim was swept down there, all hope would be gone.

Prince Chululongkorn slid down the white elephant's big trunk and held out his hand. But he could not reach her, and Tuptim was washed away!

And then the Prince was, too!

39

Tusker and the royal white elephant carried Louis and Moonshee to safety.

Meanwhile, the King, who was flying in his hot air balloon, had spotted his son.

"Son! No!!" he cried as he watched the Prince being swept down the river.

Frantically, the King gestured to Rama. The royal panther hopped onto a bicycle that turned a small propeller. With his teeth, Rama pulled a string, which opened a valve that released air from the balloon. The balloon began to lower toward the river.

As the balloon sank lower and lower, it moved dangerously close to the sharp, jutting rocks. At the last moment, the King leaned out and grabbed his son.

"Father, *Tuptim*!" Prince Chululongkorn pleaded with his father.

The King looked at the rocks. He knew that if they stayed down any longer, they would crash. His Royal Highness drew in a deep breath. "Down!" he ordered Rama.

Rama gulped, but let more air out of the balloon. The King reached out, and finally pulled Tuptim in to safety!

The Kralahome, who was watching the rescue scene in his gong, was furious. "I *hate* happy endings!" he cried.

But the Kralahome refused to give in. "It's not over yet!" He raced out of his chamber. He had another evil plan.

Anna and Sir Edward were standing on the balcony. She was happy to see Louis and Moonshee riding on the elephants, heading back to the palace. Suddenly, Anna noticed something. It was the Kralahome.

"What's he doing?" Anna wondered. Then she gasped. The truth dawned upon her. The King was heading back to the palace in his hot air balloon, and the Kralahome was planning to fire a rocket at him!

Anna raced up the stairs as fast as she could. But the Kralahome reached the top of the stairs first and slammed the big iron gate in Anna's face.

"You're too late!" he seethed at Anna as he turned the key.

The Kralahome lit the rocket's fuse and the rocket streaked toward the King's balloon.

"Nooo!" Anna cried from outside the room.

The King saw the rocket coming. Bravely, he stepped in front of the others to shield them. The rocket hit the balloon, and the balloon began to fall.

"Jump!" the ruler commanded as they came close to a calm lake, just by the palace.

Tuptim, Prince Chululongkorn, and Rama jumped to safety.

But just as His Royal Highness was about to follow, the Kralahome lit the main fuse for the rest of the fireworks display. His aim was true — he hit the King's hot air balloon. It dropped like a rock.

The Kralahome sighed with satisfaction. "Good-bye, Your Majesty."

44

Anna rushed down the stairs. A crowd had formed around where the King lay, motionless.

Anna knelt next to the King and reached out to touch his forehead. Tears began to form in her eyes.

Suddenly, the King's eyes snapped open. "*I* will say when is time to cry!" Through her tears, Anna laughed with relief.

The next day, everyone gathered in the King's bedroom.

"Mrs. Anna, take notes from man to be next King," the ruler said, pointing toward Prince Chululongkorn.

Startled, the Prince stared at his father.

"Suppose you are King," His Highness said to Prince Chululongkorn. "What would you do?"

The Prince hesitated. Then he said, "I would let everyone have books. And nobody should have to bow like toads. And everyone would have the freedom to marry who they want."

Just then, Tuptim entered the room. She was dressed like a princess.

The King looked at her and agreed. "Why should royal Prince have less rights than anyone else?"

Tuptim clasped her hands, tears of joy in her eyes. She was going to marry her beloved.

THE KRALAHOME'S PUNISHMENT

But not everyone was happy. The Kralahome, who had been caught, had been punished, put to work cleaning the elephant stables. And Master Little was in charge.

Tusker and his father, the royal white elephant, grinned with satisfaction as they watched the Kralahome and Master Little work.

"Haven't they heard of elephant litter?" the Kralahome grumbled. Furious, he tried to kick Tusker, but instead he slipped and fell into the smelly mess.

"One good thing about the new job, O Soiled One . . . I have a tall, stupid assistant," Master Little said.

SHALL WE DANCE?

When the King recovered, he summoned Anna to the great ballroom.
"Mrs. Anna, you have been a very difficult woman," he began.
Anna started to object, but the King stopped her. He had a gift for her.
Anna looked out the window. There, outside the palace walls, was a little brick cottage. The King had finally given her a home of her own!
Then the King said, "At banquet, we didn't dance."
Anna laughed and took the King's outstretched hand. She sang:

Shall we dance?
On a bright cloud of music shall we fly?
Shall we dance?
Shall we then say "good night" and mean "good-bye"?
Or, perchance,
When the last little star has left the sky,
Shall we still be together
With our arms around each other
And shall you be my new romance?
On the clear understanding
That this kind of thing can happen,
Shall we dance?
         Shall we dance?
                 Shall we dance?

Anna and the King danced together — they danced, and danced!

48